ParaNorman

LAIKA

Little, Brown and Company

Hachette Book Group
237 Park Avenue, New York, NY 10017
Visit our website at www.lb-kids.com

Little, Brown and Company is a division of Hachette Book Group, Inc.
The Little, Brown name and logo are trademarks of Hachette Book Group, Inc.

First Edition: July 2012

ISBN 978-0-316-20989-2

10 9 8 7 6 5 4 3 2

CW

Printed in the United States of America

ParaNorman

Attack of the Pilgrim Zombies!

Adapted by **Annie Auerbach**

Based on the animated feature screenplay
by **Chris Butler**

LITTLE, BROWN AND COMPANY

NEW YORK BOSTON

Norman Babcock does normal things, like go to school, avoid Alvin the bully, take out the garbage, watch zombie movies, and argue with his older sister, Courtney.

But there is one thing about Norman that is not normal.
Norman can talk to ghosts!

"Hi, Grandma," says Norman.

"Tell your dad to turn up the heat! My feet are like ice,"
says Grandma.

Tonight, Norman is in the town graveyard. He was told there is a curse upon the town—and only *he* can stop the dead from coming back to life.

Norman isn't too sure he can do this—but he knows he has to try. The whole town depends on him.

"Hello?" he calls into the dark cemetery. He hears a crack behind him....

"Hey, ghost nerd! Whatcha doing out here?" It's Alvin! He saw Norman heading into the woods and decided to tag along and tease him.

"Get out of here, Alvin! Before it's too late!" yells Norman.

Suddenly there is a bright flash of lightning in the sky!
A rumble of thunder shakes the trees!

"What is *that*?" Alvin exclaims, pointing up at the clouds.

The roiling sky is forming the shape of a witch's face!

"It's the curse!" cries Norman.

The ground begins to shake violently. The headstones shift in the dirt and crack.

Right before their eyes, a skeletal hand bursts up from the grave!

"*Aaaaaaaaaaah!*" scream Alvin and Norman.

Then, more and more body parts
push up through the dirt—and
zombies rise from their graves!

Ragged, rotten, and moaning,
the zombies look old-fashioned.
They look like Pilgrims!

One zombie looks at
Norman. Then he throws
back his head and lets
out a long, scary howl.

"Make it stop right now!" Alvin pleads. "I'm way too awesome to be eaten!"

Norman realizes it's too late to stop the curse—the zombies are already here! And Norman isn't interested in sticking around to talk to them. The two boys decide to run for their lives!

"Help! Zombies!" cries Norman. They wave down a van coming toward them on the road.

It's Norman's sister, Courtney! She has rounded up Norman's friend Neil and Neil's brother, Mitch, to help find her brother—only so *she* won't get in trouble. Norman and Alvin jump into the van.

"Norman, what's going on?" asks Courtney, terrified to see Pilgrim zombies shuffling toward the van.

"Just so you know, I totally saved Norman's life and I can totally save yours, too," Alvin says dreamily to Courtney.

Neil rolls his eyes.

"Guys! Maybe we should actually drive away—now!" yells Norman, just as a zombie pops his head into the van.

The gang races back to town, but the Pilgrim zombies follow them!

Everyone in Blithe Hollow takes to the streets, ready for a zombie fight. But the zombies are more scared than the people are! The zombies have never seen bright neon lights or machines that dispense candy or girls in short skirts!

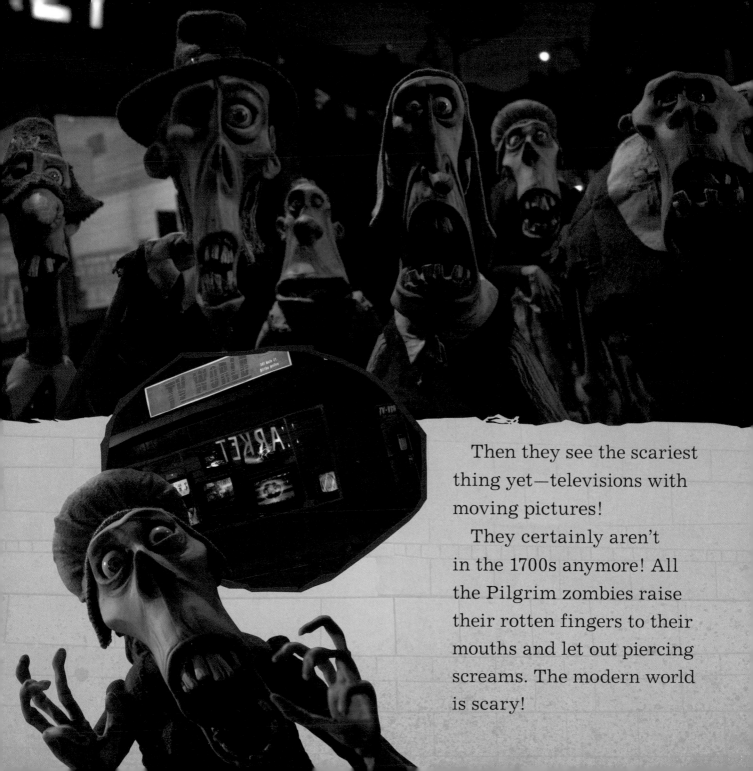

Then they see the scariest thing yet—televisions with moving pictures!

They certainly aren't in the 1700s anymore! All the Pilgrim zombies raise their rotten fingers to their mouths and let out piercing screams. The modern world is scary!

The townspeople are too scared themselves to realize that the zombies are scared, too.

"What should we do? They're disgusting!" yells one woman.

"Why don't we hit them in the head?" asks a man.

The townspeople start to form a mob.

Meanwhile, Norman and the gang sneak into the Town
Hall to hide.

"This is turning into the *most* fun ever," says Courtney
sarcastically.

"I can't believe zombies take over the world, and we're
hiding in this boring building," says Alvin. "Can't we go
across the street to the video store?"

Norman realizes he can't keep running. It's his job to save the town—no one else's.

"I don't need anyone's help," he tells the gang. "I can do this on my own."

Norman looks at his sister, Courtney. "You only came along so you wouldn't get in trouble with Mom and Dad," he accuses her.

"That's a pretty fair assessment," she agrees. Courtney leads everyone else out of the room.

Norman is alone. Just then, the zombies break into the Town Hall!

Norman shakes in his tennis shoes as they approach. The lead zombie leans over him with his eyeballs rolling around in their sockets. He raises a bony finger and points to Norman.

Then he opens his mouth, showing his rotting teeth. . . .

"Heeeeeelp…uuuuuus," he moans.

Norman stares in shock. He never quite realized it before, but because he can talk to ghosts, he can also talk to the dead—including zombies!

"Wh-what? Help you?" asks Norman. "You don't want to eat me?"

The zombie shakes his head. "You must stop this." The Pilgrim zombie explains that the curse is not on the town—it's on the *zombies*. Long ago, a witch cast the curse upon them in revenge. Now they just want to rest in peace.

"We were wrong in treating the witch so badly,"
says the zombie. "You have to talk to her for us."
Norman knows what he has to do!

Norman realizes he has to persuade the town to leave the zombies alone!

He goes outside and stands next to his sister, Neil, Mitch, and Alvin. "Hi, guys," he says. "I really need your help." The zombies come out and stand behind them.

The crowd is angry. "Get them before they eat us!" one woman shouts.

"For Pete's sake, does it look like anyone's trying to eat you?" Courtney yells back. "Right now, we just need to listen to my brother."

"The zombies are just people…or at least they used to be," pleads Norman. "They did something really mean in the past and were cursed. The curse isn't about them hurting you, but you hurting them!"

That silences the mob. Slowly, they lower their weapons—the spatulas and mixers and torches.

A little girl steps forward and offers one of the zombies his arm back. The Pilgrim zombie is scared at first, but then he smiles at the little girl.

Everyone is happy for a brief moment.

Then the sky darkens, and a
storm rages through the town.
Everyone can hear the cackling of a witch!

"I think you made the witch angry," says Neil.

"What do we do now, zombie slayer?" asks Alvin.

"Come on, everyone. Let's go talk to the witch!" cries Norman.

And another adventure begins....